The Berenstain Bears
and the

PERFECT CRIME

(Almost)

by the Berenstains

A BIG CHAPTER BOOK™

Random House New York

www.randomhouse.com/kids/
www.berenstainbears.com/

Library of Congress Cataloging-in-Publication Data
Berenstain, Stan, 1923–

The Berenstain Bears and the perfect crime (almost) / by the Berenstains.
   p. cm. — (A big chapter book)

SUMMARY: The Bear Detectives investigate the theft of a valuable historical document on the eve of Bear Country's bicentennial.

ISBN 0-679-88943-4 (trade). — ISBN 0-679-98943-9 (lib. bdg.)

[1.   Bears—Fiction.   2.   Mystery   and   detective   stories]
I. Berenstain, Jan, 1923–   . II. Title.   III. Series: Berenstain, Stan, 1923-
Big chapter book.

PZ7.B4483Bejop   1998   [Fic]—dc21   98-10031

Printed in the United States of America   10 9 8 7 6 5 4 3 2 1

BIG CHAPTER BOOKS is a trademark of Berenstain Enterprises, Inc.

IT COULDN'T HAVE COME AT A BETTER TIME!

That's what the cubs think when they find a historic document at school just days before Bear Country's two-hundredth birthday. But on the eve of the big bicentennial celebration Ferdy Factual's sharp eyes spot something strange in General George Grizzington's signature.

Is the historic find a fake? Or has the real document been stolen and *replaced* with a fake?

Contents

Chapter 1
Bear Country's Two-Hundredth

Every spring, Bear Country's citizens cele-
brated Bear Country Independence Day
with a host of festivities. In Beartown, for
instance, the day's events would start in the
town square, where Mayor Horace J. Honeypot would give a long, boring speech
about freedom, democracy, and the Bear

Country way. Then came the fun. Bears dressed as soldiers from the Revolutionary Bear War would march down Main Street, led by Mr. Honeycomb, Bear Country School's principal, dressed as the nation's first president, George Grizzington. Behind Mr. Honeycomb would be Mervyn "Bullhorn" Grizzmeyer, Bear Country School's vice principal, dressed as Bearjamin Franklin, Bear Country's first secretary of state. And directly behind Mr. Grizzmeyer would come the Bear Country School

Marching Band, playing patriotic songs from long ago. In the evening, folks would gather in the fields near Birder's Woods to watch a spectacular fireworks show.

But one year everyone knew well ahead of time that things were going to be different on Independence Day. That's because it wasn't just *any* Independence Day that was coming up. It was extra special.

"So what's going to be so different about this Independence Day?" Sister Bear asked her brother as they walked down the main hall of Bear Country School on their way to class. It was just a few mornings before the big day.

"Everything'll be twice as big as usual," said Brother. "Mayor Honeypot's speech will be twice as long and twice as boring. The parade will go down Elm Street as well as Main Street. And the fireworks display will be twice as spectacular."

"Just because it's the whaddya-call-it? *Centennial?*"

"No," said Cousin Fred, who often read the dictionary for fun. "The centennial happened a hundred years ago, on Bear Country's hundredth birthday. This Independence Day will be Bear Country's *two*-hundredth birthday. That's called a *bi*centennial."

"Whatever," said Sister. "Anyway, it'll be fun. I wish the celebration started today."

"In a way, it does," said Brother. "Remember Mr. Dweebish, the history professor from Big Bear University?"

"Sure," said Sister. "I was in his class on Foundations of Democracy last year. He was great."

"Well, he's coming back to Bear Country School for three days of lectures about George Grizzington, in honor of the bicentennial," said Brother. "He'll be here sometime this morning."

"Cool!" said Sister. "It'll be great to see him again."

But Mr. Dweebish wasn't the only one returning to Bear Country School that morning. Hurrying down the hall came Mr. Honeycomb, just back from a week-long principals' conference.

"Uh-oh," said Fred. "Honeycomb's back. He always gets back from those conferences with some kind of a bee in his bonnet."

"I wonder what's buzzing this time," said Sister.

"Depends on what kind of conference it was," said Brother. "But we'll know that soon enough."

Mr. Grizzmeyer had just emerged from his office and was heading down the hall toward the cubs. He and Mr. Honeycomb were within earshot of the cubs when their paths met. "Well, Mr. H," said Grizzmeyer, "how was the efficiency conference?"

"Excellent," said Mr. Honeycomb. "It made me resolve to honor the bicentennial by improving Bear Country School's efficiency. We'll start by eliminating all waste. I'm about to get on the public address system and cancel classes for this morning. All students will participate in a schoolwide cleanup." He pointed to a bulletin board on

the hallway wall. "Look at that mess! I'll bet most of those notices are years old. They're *waste*, Mr. G. *Eliminate* them!" He strode off toward his office.

Before the public address system had uttered so much as a crackle, Mr. Grizzmeyer had ordered Brother, Sister, and Fred to clear off the bulletin board. In fact, he had put them in charge of clearing off *all* the bulletin boards in the school.

Chapter 2
An Incredible Discovery

Clearing off all the school bulletin boards was a big job. Fortunately, the cubs picked up a couple of helpers along the way: Queenie McBear and Ferdy Factual. By the time the bell rang for morning recess, they had filled five big plastic trash bags with old notices and announcements. They dragged the bags to Mr. Honeycomb's office and knocked.

"It's open," called Mr. Honeycomb.

Brother opened the door and patted his

trash bag. "We're done, Mr. H," he said. "Where should we take the bags?"

"I'll call Grizzly Gus on the intercom," said Mr. Honeycomb. Gus was the school janitor. "He'll bring his trash cart and take them away. Are you sure you got all the bulletin boards?"

"Yep," said Brother. "All the hallway and

classroom boards, and the big one in the cafeteria, too."

"What about the teachers' lounge?" asked Mr. Honeycomb.

"Teachers' lounge?" said Fred. "Is there one in there?"

"Of course," said Mr. Honeycomb. "And it's the worst of all. I can't remember the last time it was cleaned off. I'll have Gus bring you a couple more trash bags."

"But what about recess?" said Queenie.

"You'll just have to work quickly so you don't miss all of it," said Mr. Honeycomb. "It'll be a good lesson in *efficiency*."

The cubs got new bags from Gus and headed for the teachers' lounge. "I'll be glad when Mr. H gets off this efficiency kick," grumbled Queenie as they walked. "Who would have thought we'd start the bicentennial celebration by missing recess?"

"Actually," said Ferdy, "one could argue that recess should be eliminated altogether. As a matter of efficiency."

"How's that?" said Queenie.

"It's a *waste* of time," said Ferdy.

"Only if your idea of relaxing between classes is reading an atomic physics textbook," sneered Queenie.

Moments later, the cubs were standing before the bulletin board in the teachers' lounge. None of them had ever set foot in the lounge before. Ordinarily, it was off-limits to cubs. Now they studied it carefully, the way cubs do in a place reserved for grownups. What they took in was a strange combination of old and new, of antique and modern. There were modern tables and chairs, a coffee maker, snack and soda machines. But the room itself was anything but modern.

"Wow," said Sister. "This doesn't look anything like our classrooms."

"That's because the classrooms have been redone several times," said Fred. "But this room hasn't. It's the original town meeting room, and it hasn't changed since Bear Country School was first built, except for some new coats of paint. I know because I just finished a history project on Bear Country School."

"How old is Bear Country School?" asked Brother.

"Over two hundred years old," said Fred. "It was the first public building in Beartown."

"I'll bet that bulletin board was the first one in Beartown, too," said Queenie. "Just look at it."

Along the top of it, peeking out from behind a thick coat of notices and

14

announcements, was a wooden edge, all chipped and splintered. The teachers' lounge bulletin board was just that: an old wooden board.

"We'd better get to work," said Brother. "These notices must be three inches thick!"

The first layer of notices was from that year. But soon the cubs were into years past. And after a while, they were into years *long* past.

15

"Hey, look at this one!" said Sister. " 'Gert Grizzly will show her award-winning sixth-grade project, "The War on Germs," to faculty and staff on Friday, October 25, after school.' That's Dr. Gert!"

"Already on her way to becoming a doctor," said Ferdy.

"Whoa!" said Queenie. "Get a load of this! 'Actual Factual has received a one-day suspension for making a rotten-egg smell in chemistry.' Hey, Ferdy, that's your uncle—on *his* way to becoming a scientist."

"May I have that?" said Ferdy.

"Sure," said Queenie. "What do you want it for?"

"It could come in handy next time I need a favor from Uncle Actual," said Ferdy with a grin.

Before long, the cubs had come across notices from a hundred years earlier and

more. Some famous names popped up. Horace Grizzly, the great journalist, was to give a lecture in the town meeting room. General Ulysses S. Bear would talk about military strategy during the War Between the Clans. There was even an announcement of the Bear Country centennial festivities, including a speech in the town square by Mayor Hector J. Honeypot, Horace J. Honeypot's great-grandfather.

Some of the old notices were printed, others handwritten in ink. All were faded, on paper yellowed by time. The cubs were fascinated. They stared long and hard at each new discovery.

"Something tells me we shouldn't throw these really old ones away," said Brother after a while.

"Of course not," said Ferdy. "They should go straight to the Bearsonian Institution. There may well be a place for them in its historical wing."

At last, there was only one notice left. Its corners were stuck to the board with wax—very old wax—and it was right in the center

of the board, as if it had been the very first notice ever displayed there. It was so old that it was covered with brown blotches and its edges were jagged and uneven. Even so, the fine, flowing handwriting on it was

Hear ye! Hear ye!
citizenf of Beartown village!
I hereby fummon thee
to the town meeting room of
the village fchool, on the
evening of May the
twelfth, at the hour of feven
o'clock to difcuff
Life, Liberty, and the purfuit
of happineff.

General George Brizzington LLL

plainly visible. Craning their necks, the cubs pressed forward to read it.

"*Fummon* thee?" said Queenie.

"*Feven* o'clock?" said Brother.

"*Purfuit* of *Happineff*?" said Queenie.

"That's how they wrote two hundred years ago," said Fred. "They made s's look like f's."

"Oh, my goodness!" cried Ferdy. "The chap who wrote this signed his name at the bottom. And look who it was!"

At the bottom of the announcement, as clear as day, were the words *General George Grizzington.*

"George Grizzington!" said Sister. "The father of Bear Country!"

"The first president of Bear Country!" said Queenie.

"But he wrote this when he was still *General* George Grizzington, commander of the

Revolutionary Bear Army," Fred pointed out.

"Do you think it's real?" said Brother.

"Of course!" said Fred. "Just look at it."

As always, Ferdy was skeptical. "Don't be so easily fooled," he yawned. "It's obviously a prank. A bicentennial prank. Too-Tall probably did it."

"Oh, please!" groaned Queenie. "Too-Tall isn't *smart* enough to pull a stunt like this. His idea of a bicentennial prank is throwing water bombs at the marching band!"

Ferdy put his chin in his hand and eyed the notice again. "Hmm," he said. "You may have a point there."

When the bell rang, ending recess, the cubs didn't even notice. They were still completely engrossed in the amazing document on the ancient bulletin board.

Chapter 3
A Wonderful Dream

The cubs were still staring at the notice on the bulletin board when the door of the teachers' lounge opened and in walked a grownup wearing a gray suit, a gray hat, and thick glasses. "Well, cubs, I'm back!" he said brightly. Then he frowned. "But what are you doing in *here?*"

"Mr. Dweebish!" said Brother. "Mr. Grizzmeyer told us to clear off this bulletin board. And look what we just found!"

Mr. Dweebish set down his briefcase and went to the bulletin board. He read the notice, blinked his eyes, took off his glasses to clean them with a handkerchief, and read the notice again. His knees started to shake. Brother quickly pushed a chair behind him so he could sit down. "Are you okay, Mr. Dweebish?" he asked.

"Yes, yes, I'm all right," sighed the teacher. "Just overcome with emotion. It's incredible! Astonishing! It must have been posted here in the months leading up to the Declaration of Bear Independence, the very event whose bicentennial we are about to celebrate. And to think that it has been sitting there, forgotten, all these years!"

"So you think it's the real thing?" said Fred.

"Oh, yes," said Mr. Dweebish. "Of course, we'll have to have it authenticated by a document expert."

"Authenticated?" said Sister.

"Fred," said Mr. Dweebish, "how about you doing the honors? As I recall, you were always quick with a definition."

"Authenticate," said Fred. *"To establish as genuine."*

"That's correct," said Mr. Dweebish. "In

our history department at Big Bear University, we have a document expert who can do the job. Unfortunately, he's way up in Polar Bear City at the moment, authenticating some letters of Admiral Beary's that were recently found buried near the Northern Pole. Such a shame!"

"Why is it a shame?" asked Brother.

"Because I'd dearly love to get this document authenticated in time for the bicentennial. We can't in good conscience put it on public display before it has been properly authenticated."

"What an event *that* would be!" said Brother. "General George Grizzington's handwritten notice on display for the bicentennial!"

"Folks would flock to Beartown from all over Bear Country to see it!" said Fred.

"It would really put Beartown on the map," said Ferdy.

"And it would be great for our shops and hotels and restaurants!" added Queenie.

"Yes, it's a wonderful dream," said Mr. Dweebish. "But no more than that."

"Don't you know any other document experts?" asked Ferdy.

"I'm afraid not, cubs," said Mr. Dweebish sadly.

Chapter 4
Cookin' Up a Scheme

All over Bear Country, bears were busy getting ready for the bicentennial festivities. But some weren't even thinking about the bicentennial. Ralph Ripoff, for example. Ralph was Beartown's leading crook and swindler. He hadn't had a successful swindle in a while, and he was desperate to come up with one.

"Squawk, my friend," Ralph said to his pet parrot as he settled into his comfy chair in the living room of his houseboat, "let's go surfing."

"Surfing! Surfing!" said Squawk.

Ralph picked up the remote and switched on the TV. He often channel-surfed when he was cooking up a scheme. It seemed to help his thoughts flow more freely. Sometimes he even saw something on TV that gave him an idea.

First, he landed on the Shopping Channel. "This channel is a real gold mine," he said. "I've got all kinds of schemes to swindle it, but none of them is foolproof."

"Foolproof! Foolproof!" said Squawk.

Ralph pressed the remote until he hit a news channel. Tom Bearclaw, the well-known anchorbear, was speaking with great excitement. "This just in! An announcement for a meeting was discovered today at Bear Country School in Beartown. But not just *any* announcement. It appears to have been written and signed by General George Grizzington just over two hundred years ago. Professor Dweebish, a historian from

Big Bear University, believes that the notice was posted by the father of Bear Country himself on the bulletin board of what is now the teachers' lounge, during his campaign to draw up the Declaration of Bear Independence. We go now to Beartown, where our correspondent, Gale Goodbear, is with Professor Dweebish. Gale?"

Gale Goodbear appeared on the screen. Next to her was Mr. Dweebish, who seemed to be trying to keep his face from breaking into a silly grin. In the background was the bulletin board in the teachers' lounge, with the Grizzington document clearly visible.

GOODBEAR: "Mr. Dweebish, are you certain the document is authentic?"
DWEEBISH: "Oh, yes. But that's just my personal opinion. It should really be authenticated by an expert."

GOODBEAR: "And when will the public be allowed to view this great find in person?"

DWEEBISH: "Unfortunately, not until after the bicentennial, when the university's document expert returns from Polar Bear City to authenticate it."

GOODBEAR: "And what will be done with the document in the long run?"

DWEEBISH: "Squire Grizzly, the well-known Beartown billionaire and collector of historic artifacts, has expressed a keen interest in buying it for his personal collection. However, Mayor Honeypot and the town council will almost surely donate the document to the Bearsonian Institution, to be put on permanent public display there."

Hmm, thought Ralph. So Squire Grizzly wants to buy the thing. Well, that isn't sur-

prising, considering his lifelong passion for historic artifacts. He must be absolutely dying to get his greedy little hands on that document...

Squawk was sensitive to Ralph's moods. He could tell that his master was onto something big. "Cookin' up a scheme! Cookin' up a scheme!" he squawked.

"You've got that right, good buddy!" said Ralph, leaping to his feet and dashing to the telephone. "And this time, it'll make us rich!"

Ralph punched in a phone number. "Hello, Fritz? It's me, Ralph. Ralph *Ripoff*. Sure, I know it's been a long time. But I'm not the kind of guy who forgets an old buddy when the opportunity of a lifetime arises—wait, don't hang up! Yes, I know you went straight—antiques business, an honest living, and all that—but wait till you hear the scheme I've cooked up. All it involves is a few hours of your expert work. And I already have a buyer in mind! We'll make *millions...*"

Chapter 5
A Perfect Plan

The next morning, the cubs found Chief Bruno guarding the front entrance to Bear Country School. The Grizzington document was so valuable that no strangers were allowed into the building. Officer Marguerite was stationed at the back entrance.

Brother, Sister, and Cousin Fred were heading for class when they decided to stop by the teachers' lounge for a quick look at the Grizzington document. They opened the door a crack and peeked in.

"Hey, close that door!" snapped Miss Glitch, who was sitting at one of the tables inside. "This lounge is off-limits to cubs!"

"It's all right, Miss Glitch," said Mr. Dweebish. "They're the ones who discovered the document. Come on in, cubs."

Once inside, the cubs saw that Grizzly Gus was chipping away with a chisel at the wax that held the document to the bulletin board as Mr. Dweebish looked on.

"What are you doing?" asked Brother.

"Great news, cubs!" said Mr. Dweebish. "Last night I got a call from a document expert who offered to authenticate our document for free. His name is Max McFlurish, and he lives just a few miles away in Bearville. I'm about to take the document to his antiques shop right now."

"That's great!" said Sister. "Now we can put the document on display for the bicentennial!"

Mr. Dweebish nodded. He was beaming. "I plan to invite the public to a viewing right here in the teachers' lounge after my final lecture on George Grizzington in the school auditorium tomorrow afternoon. Gus will stick the document back onto the bulletin board with wax so the public can see it just as it was when you found it."

"But why can't the expert authenticate it here?" asked Fred.

"He has to run a number of complicated tests on it," Mr. Dweebish explained. "Chemical tests to determine the age of the paper, computer analysis of the handwriting, and so on. He has a special laboratory for the authentication of documents in the back room of his antiques shop."

"Gee," said Brother. "You'd better be careful, Mr. Dweebish. It's such a valuable document..."

"Don't worry," said Mr. Dweebish. He pointed to an object resting on the nearest table. "The document will be locked in that steel briefcase at all times, except during the authentication process."

"But what if someone steals the case?" asked Brother.

"Then they'll have to steal *me,* too," said Mr. Dweebish. He went over to the briefcase and held up a chain attached to it. At the free end of the chain was a handcuff. "Because I will be securely handcuffed to it."

"But what if they find the key to the handcuff on you?" said Sister.

"Not a chance," said Mr. Dweebish. "Because the key will be in the possession of Chief Bruno, who will drive me to Bearville and back in his squad car."

"Sounds like a perfect plan," said Brother.

"Thank you," said Mr. Dweebish. "The Grizzington document should be back in its proper place before the end of the school day."

With the utmost care, Gus took down the document, put it in a folder, and placed the folder in the steel briefcase. Mr. Dweebish then slipped the handcuff onto his wrist and closed it. The cubs followed him into the hall. "Good luck!" they called as Mr. Dweebish headed for the front entrance, where Chief Bruno was waiting.

"Thanks, cubs!" Mr. Dweebish called back. "But I won't need it! Nothing can go wrong!"

Chapter 6
Bicentennial City

All day long, the cubs kept looking out of their classroom windows at the school parking lot, hoping to see Chief Bruno's squad car return with Mr. Dweebish and his steel briefcase. But when the final bell rang, ending the school day, the chief's car was still a no-show.

"What do you suppose happened to Chief Bruno and Mr. Dweebish?" said Fred to

Brother as they walked with Sister down the hall to the front entrance. Brother just shrugged.

"Remember when Mr. Dweebish said, 'Nothing can go wrong'?" said Sister. "Well, something *did*."

"How could it, Sis?" asked Brother. "What about the steel briefcase? And Chief Bruno protecting it?"

"I don't know how it happened, but it did," replied Sister. She stopped when they reached the front steps. "I'm gonna wait right here for them."

"Hey, here they come!" said Fred.

Chief Bruno's squad car pulled into the parking lot. Mr. Dweebish and the chief got out and headed for the school entrance. Mr. Dweebish was still handcuffed to the steel briefcase. And he was smiling. The cubs ran down the steps to greet them.

"What took you so long?" said Sister. "We were worried sick about you!"

"Sorry, cubs," said Mr. Dweebish. "Max McFlurish is a real stickler for accuracy. He ran every test twice to make sure the results were the same."

"And what *were* the results?" asked Sister.

"Can't you tell from our faces?" said Chief Bruno, beaming.

"Hurray!" cried the cubs. "It's authentic!"

"That's right, cubs," said Mr. Dweebish. "The George Grizzington document is genuine. I'm going to have Gus put it back on the bulletin board right this minute. And tomorrow afternoon we'll have the first public viewing."

"Better start getting the word out," said Fred.

"I called the newspapers and the TV and radio stations from Bearville," said Mr. Dweebish. "This is going to do more than just put Beartown on the map, you know. In years to come, I daresay, Beartown will be known as the Bicentennial City."

Chapter 7
Real or Rotten?

With the public announcement of the authenticity of the George Grizzington document, excitement mounted in Beartown. Town officials and merchants prepared frantically for the coming crush of bicentennial visitors. Meanwhile, on the day after the announcement, at the end of the school day, Beartown folks packed the school auditorium to hear Mr. Dweebish's final bicentennial lecture on General George Grizzington's famed crossing of the Delabear River. Then they filed through the teachers' lounge to get their first look at the recently discovered document. Many lingered at the bulletin board, as if communing with history. Squire Grizzly, that great lover of historic artifacts, was so fascinated by the document that he even examined it with a magnifying glass.

"What's wrong, Ferdy?" asked Brother. "You look like you just ate a rotten apple." The two cubs had filed past the document with the crowd and were now walking down the hall toward the front entrance.

"That's because I may have just seen a rotten document," said Ferdy.

"Rotten document?" said Brother. "What do you mean?"

"Rotten as in *phony*," said Ferdy. "The Grizzington document. There's something funny about it."

"Funny?" said Brother. "You didn't say that when we found it."

"I know," said Ferdy. "But there's something different about it now. I can't quite put my finger on what it is. I need another look. Let's get back in line. Come on."

The cubs hurried back to the end of the line. But just as they got there, Mr. Dweebish stepped in front of them. "Sorry, cubs," he said. "I've just cut off the line. Closing time."

"But I have to get another look," said Ferdy. "There's something wrong with the document. It might be a fake!"

Mr. Dweebish laughed. "It looks fine to everyone else," he said. "Besides, it's been authenticated by an expert. Now go home and have dinner. That's what *I'm* going to do. And stop worrying."

Ferdy looked deeply troubled as he left school with Brother. "If I'm right," he said, "we have a disaster on our hands. Beartown will be the laughingstock of all Bear Country if we put a phony document on display for the bicentennial."

"But you heard Mr. Dweebish," said Brother. "It was authenticated by an expert—"

"We need to investigate," said Ferdy. "Call a meeting of the Bear Detectives! Please! At least hear me out!"

Brother considered this for a while. "Well, okay," he said finally. "Meet us at the Burger Bear for shakes after dinner. But you'd better be convincing. The Bear Detectives don't take false alarms lightly."

Chapter 8
Temporary Bear Detective

At the Burger Bear that evening, Ferdy repeated his suspicions to Brother, Sister, Fred, and Lizzy. He urged them to investigate. He was so persuasive that the Bear Detectives were inclined to do it.

"That'll be easy," said Lizzy. "Tomorrow is the bicentennial, and the teachers' lounge will be open to the public all day. We can have a look at the document then."

"No!" said Ferdy. "By then it will be too late. We can't allow a phony document to be put on display!"

"What are you suggesting?" said Fred. "That we break into school tonight?"

"Exactly," said Ferdy.

"Gee, I don't know," said Brother. "That would be illegal."

"Can you think of another way to get a look at the document before tomorrow?" said Ferdy.

The Bear Detectives looked at one another. They shook their heads.

"Well," said Ferdy, "that decides it. The only thing we have to do first is get some help from the break-in department." He slid out of the booth, went over to where Too-Tall and his gang were sitting, and whispered something in Too-Tall's ear. Too-

Tall grinned and got up and followed Ferdy back to the Bear Detectives' booth.

"No sweat," said Too-Tall. "I could break into school in my sleep. Follow me."

"Wait," said Sister. "We have to swear you both in as temporary Bear Detectives. You have to say the secret Bear Detective Oath. Too-Tall first."

"Not me," said Too-Tall. "I ain't investigating. I'm just breaking and entering."

"Well, I guess that excuses you," said Sister. "Okay, Ferdy. Raise your right hand and repeat after me: *I, Ferdy Factual, do solemnly swear to work my hardest to solve every case.*"

Ferdy repeated the oath, then said, "That's all?"

"Well, we're not making you president of Bear Country, you know," said Sister.

Doing their best to look as if nothing out of the ordinary were about to happen, the cubs left the Burger Bear and headed for school.

Chapter 9
A Shocking Discovery

Afraid of being seen near school, Too-Tall and the Bear Detectives made their approach through the woods beyond the football field. They half expected to find Chief Bruno and Officer Marguerite still guarding the entrances. But the school was deserted.

"Piece o' cake," said Too-Tall. "We'll use the back entrance."

The deadbolt on the back door was no match for Too-Tall. Inside in no time, the cubs made their way along the darkened hallway to the teachers' lounge. Too-Tall picked the lock on the door and let the cubs in.

"Okay," he said, "you're on your own now. Remember: If you get caught, *I* was at the Burger Bear all evening." And, with that, he silently made his way back down the hall.

Brother found the light switch, and the Bear Detectives turned their attention to the bulletin board. There was the George

Grizzington document, right in the center, where Grizzly Gus had reattached it with wax. The cubs approached it for a closer look.

"Seems okay to me," said Brother.

"Me too," said Fred.

"Me three," said Sister.

But Lizzy, who had especially sharp eyes, spent a long time squinting at the document. "There's something odd about it," she said. "I think it's the signature."

"That's it!" cried Ferdy. "The signature! Look at the last three letters!"

"Okay, I'm looking," said Brother. "Tell me what I'm seeing."

"The *ton* in *Grizzington* was written with a different pen than the rest of the document!" said Ferdy.

"Yeah," said Fred. "I see it. Maybe he broke his quill pen at the *g* and had to finish

Fountain pen

Quill pen

the signature with a different one."

"I don't think so," said Ferdy.

"Why not?" said Sister. "Even George Grizzington could have broken a pen, couldn't he?"

"Of course," said Ferdy. "But I guarantee you that if he ever did break a pen in the middle of a word, he did not then switch to a *fountain* pen!"

The cubs now looked so closely at the signature that their noses almost pressed against it.

"You're right!" cried Fred. "The *ton* was written with a fountain pen!"

"Yep," said Brother. "I see it, too."

"Then George Grizzington couldn't have

Grizzington

written it!" said Sister. "Two hundred years ago, fountain pens weren't invented yet!"

"My point precisely," said Ferdy.

"Then the document must be a forgery," said Brother.

"A *what?*" said Sister.

"*Forgery,*" said Fred. "*A phony piece of work that is claimed to be genuine.*"

"But that's not all," said Ferdy. "When we first found the document, I examined it very carefully. I'm quite certain that the signature was written entirely with a quill pen."

The cubs were silent as they struggled to grasp the full meaning of Ferdy's statement.

Finally, Brother said, "But that means that not only is this document a forgery, the *original* document has been *stolen!*"

"It certainly looks that way," said Ferdy.

"But who could have stolen it?" said Sister. "And when?"

Ferdy shrugged. "I have no idea who stole it," he said. "As to when, I can't be sure of that, either. But I do know that Grizzly Gus put it back here on the bulletin board right after Mr. Dweebish returned with it from Bearville yesterday afternoon. And it wasn't until *this* afternoon that the public viewing took place. Hence, the document was here in this room, *unguarded,* all last night."

"Oh, my gosh!" cried Sister. "This is a disaster! What are we gonna do?"

"There's only one thing to do," said Brother. "Take this forged document to the police station and show it to Chief Bruno. *Right away!*"

Chapter 10
Caught!

No sooner had the Bear Detectives slipped out the back door of the school than a pair of headlights came rushing at them out of the darkness and a car stopped just short of the steps. "Hold it right there!" boomed a familiar voice. "Put your hands in the air and don't move!"

"It's Chief Bruno," Brother said to the others. "Hey, Chief! It's just us! The Bear Detectives!"

"You heard me!" barked the chief. "Hands in the air! Pronto!"

The cubs did as they were told. Chief Bruno and Officer Marguerite got out of the squad car. "It's a good thing we installed that silent alarm today," the chief said to Officer Marguerite. He approached the cubs. "It's the perfect thing for catching cubs like you. A break-in at school sets it off, but it rings only at the police station."

"Yeah," said Officer Marguerite. "Otherwise, you cubs might have gotten away with it."

"Gotten away with *what?*" said Sister.

"With this rotten prank," said the chief. He reached out and snatched the document from Brother's raised hand. "All right, you can put your hands down now. You cubs ought to be ashamed of yourselves, stealing the Grizzington document as a prank. On the eve of the bicentennial, no less!"

"But we didn't steal the Grizzington document!" said Sister. "We stole a forgery!"

"What Sis means," said Brother, "is that we didn't steal anything. We found this forgery in the teachers' lounge and were on our way down to the station to show it to you."

"Forgery?" said Chief Bruno. "What on earth are you talking about? This document was authenticated by Max McFlurish yesterday."

"I believe someone stole it after it was authenticated," said Ferdy. "Possibly last night. And they replaced it with this forgery."

Ferdy explained how he had grown suspicious of the document's authenticity that afternoon and had persuaded the Bear Detectives to break into school to examine

it before it went on display for the bicentennial. He showed Chief Bruno where the signature had been finished with a fountain pen. But in the glare of the headlights, the chief couldn't see anything wrong with the signature. "That's the dumbest story I ever heard!" he growled.

"Take it down to the station, where you can look at it in better light!" pleaded Ferdy. "Please, Chief!"

"Funny you should say that," said Chief Bruno. "Because that's exactly where we're all headed. Cuff 'em, Marguerite!"

The cubs were shocked. So was Officer Marguerite. *"Handcuffs?"* she said. "But they're just cubs, Chief. I don't even have five pairs of handcuffs with me."

"Oh, all right," said the chief. "Get in the squad car, cubs. But don't try anything funny."

The Bear Detectives crowded into the back seat of the squad car and sat silently as Chief Bruno drove them to the police station. On the way, they passed the town square, where a grandstand and platform for Mayor Honeypot's bicentennial speech had been set up. The sight made the cubs' hearts ache. What a bicentennial *this* would be! All of Bear Country celebrating while *they* were in jail! It was a nightmare!

Chapter 11
Dweebish to the Rescue

At the station, Chief Bruno refused to examine the document again. Convinced of the cubs' guilt, he was about to lock them up when Ferdy remembered something.

"Wait, Chief!" he cried. "Before you lock us up, call Mr. Dweebish. He'll vouch for my story. This afternoon I told him I thought the document was a fake. Would I have done that if we were planning to steal it as a prank?"

Chief Bruno thought for a moment. "All right," he said. "I'll call him. But you'd better be telling the truth!"

The chief phoned Miz McGrizz's house, where Mr. Dweebish was staying. Miz McGrizz said that Mr. Dweebish had gone to bed early with a headache, but the chief said it was urgent. When Chief Bruno told the professor what the problem was, he said he would come right down. Minutes later, he burst through the station door, all out of breath. "I came as quickly as I could!" he gasped.

Chief Bruno looked him up and down and said, "I can see that." The professor's pajamas were sticking out from underneath his gray suit. "Well, can you vouch for Ferdy's story?"

"Absolutely, Chief," panted Mr. Dwee-bish. "But I laughed him off, told him it was impossible that the document was a fake. I'm not surprised the cubs felt they had to break into school to get another look at it. Let me see it, Chief."

Chief Bruno fetched a magnifying glass and, with Mr. Dweebish, examined the document. Both saw the problem instantly.

"My goodness, it's true!" said Mr. Dwee-bish. "What a remarkable forgery. We'd never have known without Ferdy's sharp eyes. Who could have stolen it? And how?"

"Obviously, it was stolen after it was authenticated," said Chief Bruno. "Probably sometime last night, before we installed the silent alarm. Tracking down the thief will be a huge job. There must be several dozen forgers who could have done it."

"Wait a minute," said Ferdy. He had come over to the document and was staring at it with intense concentration.

"What is it, son?" asked Chief Bruno.

"The document may not have been stolen *after* it was authenticated," said Ferdy.

"What do you mean?" said Mr. Dweebish. "It couldn't have been stolen *before* it was authenticated. Because then it never would have been authenticated!"

"No," admitted Ferdy. "But it *could* have been stolen *while it was being authenti-cated.*"

Mr. Dweebish's mouth fell open. He

turned to Chief Bruno. "Ferdy's right, Chief!" he said. "Do you remember how Max McFlurish asked us to wait outside his laboratory, in the antiques showroom, while he authenticated the document? He said he couldn't work properly without complete privacy. He was *alone* with that document for *hours!*"

Chief Bruno nodded. "That gave him more than enough time to forge it and switch the forgery and the original. But why would he make the mistake of finishing a two-hundred-year-old signature with a fountain pen?"

"Maybe his quill pen broke," suggested Ferdy. "He couldn't go out to look for another, because you and Mr. Dweebish were waiting outside the laboratory door. You might have been suspicious if he'd tried to leave in the middle of authenticating the document."

Chief Bruno frowned. "He'd have to be awful dumb to have just one quill pen handy for a big job like this. At any rate, we need to run a computer check on him."

Everyone crowded around the computer monitor as Officer Marguerite began typing at the keyboard. Soon the telltale words appeared on the screen. *Max McFlurish: see Fritz Braun.*

"Fritz Braun," said Chief Bruno. "That name sounds mighty familiar."

Officer Marguerite punched some more keys, and the following paragraph appeared.

Fritz Braun, also known as
Fritz the Forger.
Aliases: Fernando Furishio,
Marcus McFur, Max McFlurish.
Suspected of many cases of forgery,
convicted only once.
Served five years in
Bear Country Prison.
Known associate of Ralph Ripoff.

"Fritz the Forger!" cried Chief Bruno. "I'll bet Ralph's mixed up in this, too. Well, we've got our bear. This time, thanks to Ferdy Factual." He beamed down at the cub. "Son, you're a genius!"

For the first time that evening, Ferdy felt relaxed enough to let out one of his notorious bored yawns. "Of course I am," he replied. "Everyone knows that."

Chapter 12
They're Getting Away!

Because they had been so helpful in discovering and breaking the Case of the Forged Document, the Bear Detectives were invited by Chief Bruno to accompany Officer Marguerite and him to nab the suspects. They piled into the chief's squad car and headed for Bearville.

The car was coasting silently down the Bearville street where Fritz the Forger's shop was located when Chief Bruno suddenly switched off his headlights and pulled over to the curb. "Look up ahead," he said.

"See that car sitting in front of Fritz's shop?"

In the light from a nearby street lamp, they could see two figures in the front seat of the car. One of them was wearing a straw hat.

"It's Ralph!" said Sister.

"And I'll bet that's Fritz the Forger with him!" said Brother.

Just then the car's brake lights came on. It pulled away from the curb and headed down the street. At first, Chief Bruno didn't make a move.

"Come on, Chief!" said Lizzy. "They're getting away!"

"We don't want them to notice us," said the chief. "Especially in a squad car."

When Fritz's car was nearly out of sight, the chief turned his headlights back on and followed. They followed Fritz's car all the

way back to Beartown. They went right past the town square, with its waiting grandstand and platform, and on toward the outskirts of town. At last, Fritz's car pulled up at a wrought-iron gate.

"That's the entrance to Squire and Lady Grizzly's estate!" said Brother.

They saw Ralph lean out of the passenger window and say something to the guard. Moments later, the massive gate swung open and Fritz drove up the drive toward Grizzly Mansion.

"Fritz and Ralph must have an appointment with the squire," said Officer Marguerite. "It looks like they were expected."

"Do you think Squire Grizzly is mixed up in the theft of the document?" asked Fred.

"I can't believe that," said Brother. "I can't believe he's greedy enough to steal a historic document."

"Well, we'll soon know if he is," said Chief Bruno.

They waited until Fritz and Ralph were safely inside Grizzly Mansion, then approached the gate. The guard opened it without even questioning the chief and reached for the switch on his intercom.

"Don't!" Chief Bruno barked at him. "Don't warn anyone we're here!"

They parked behind Fritz's car, went to the porch, and rang the doorbell. Greeves, the butler, answered. His eyes widened in surprise. "Chief Bruno!" he said. "How nice to see you. I'll go tell the squire you're here."

"No need for that," said the chief. "Just take us to him."

"Very well," said Greeves. "Master is in the study with Mr. Ripoff and Mr. McFlurish. I'll show you in.

"I had no idea so many guests would be coming to the meeting," Greeves continued as he led them down the hallway to the study.

"Exactly what kind of meeting is it?" asked Chief Bruno.

"Don't you know yet?" said Greeves. "It's something about examining a historic document. The squire owns quite a few, you know."

They had reached the study. "Stand back, Greeves," whispered Chief Bruno. Then he seized the doorknob and, as the others crowded round, flung open the door.

Three shocked faces looked up at them. Squire Grizzly, Ralph Ripoff, and Fritz Braun were gathered around a table. And there on the table, in plain view, lay the missing document.

Chapter 13
The Perfect Crime?

"Chief Bruno!" said Squire Grizzly. "What are you doing here?"

"I think the better question is, what are *they* doing here?" said the chief, indicating Fritz and Ralph.

"Oh, them!" said the squire. "They're...er, uh...authenticating a document from my private collection of historic artifacts." As he spoke, he placed his body in front of the document, as if to shield it from the chief's gaze.

"Come off it, Squire," said Chief Bruno.

"Ralph Ripoff is no document expert. Besides, you told me years ago that you always have documents authenticated *before* adding them to your collection. Get out of the way!"

Squire Grizzly hesitated, but finally stepped aside.

"Just as I thought," said Chief Bruno, approaching the table. "The stolen George Grizzington document!" He turned to Fritz Braun. "By the way, we know your real name isn't Max McFlurish."

At that point, Ralph panicked. He grabbed the chief's arm and pleaded, "Please, Chief, go easy on us!"

But Fritz pulled Ralph away. "Stop that, you fool!" he whispered into Ralph's ear. "They'll never prove we stole the document. We'll get off easy. Now shut up and let me do the talking." He turned to Chief Bruno.

"Please forgive my associate. He's just afraid that Judge Gavel will give us a harsh sentence for possession of stolen property."

The chief stared at Fritz. "*Possession* of stolen property?" he said. "What about grand theft? What about the lowdown pilfering of a national treasure?"

"But we didn't steal the document," replied Fritz. "Squire Grizzly will back me up."

"All right, Squire," said Chief Bruno. "What do you know about how they got this document?"

"Just what Max told me on the phone," said the squire. "He said that he had been contacted by a forger who had stolen the Grizzington document for a well-known collector. But when the forger went to hand over the document and get paid for the job, the collector got cold feet and backed out."

"Cold feet?" Lizzy whispered to Sister. "But it's June!"

"It means he got scared," whispered Sister.

"So the forger offered Max half the money if Max would find a buyer for him— and also authenticate the document for the buyer, if necessary," continued Squire Grizzly. "Max got my name as a potential buyer from Ralph, who is an old friend of his. I asked how I could be sure the document *he* had was the original and not a clever forgery, and he told me that the last three letters of the signature on the forgery had been written with a fountain pen instead of a quill to signal the buyer that it was indeed a forgery. I went to Bear Country School this afternoon, during the public viewing of the document, and examined the signature with a magnifying glass. That satisfied me that the document was a forgery. I was about to purchase the original when you showed up."

"And you actually believed that tall tale about another forger?" said Chief Bruno. "Didn't it seem odd that a supposedly honest document expert would be contacted by

a forger? Didn't it occur to you that Max McFlurish—alias Fritz the Forger, by the way—might *himself* be the forger and thief?"

Squire Grizzly blushed. "I hate to admit it, Chief," he said, "but I was more concerned with getting my own hands on the document than with how *they* had gotten *their* hands on it."

"Well, it hardly matters that the story fooled you," said the chief. "You still knew the document was stolen, and you were going to buy it anyway. You ought to be ashamed of yourself!"

The squire hung his head. "I *am* ashamed," he said. "I let my passion for historic artifacts turn to greed. And I let my greed persuade me that because the document had already been replaced with a first-rate forgery, it would never be missed. I

could have the original all to myself, I thought, and no one would get hurt."

"A lot of Bear Country citizens almost did get hurt," said Chief Bruno. "They almost got tricked into coming to Bear Country School to see a forgery on the bicentennial!"

Squire Grizzly put his head in his hands and said nothing.

"As for you two," said Chief Bruno, turning to Ralph and Fritz, "nobody's going to believe your phony story about some mysterious forger stealing the document. I dare you to tell it to a jury."

Fritz smiled ever so slightly. "I'd be
happy to oblige you, Chief Bruno," he said.
"But I think you should hear all the details
before passing judgment. There's nothing
mysterious about the forger. It was Phil
Grizzinski, alias Phony Phil, of Big Bear
City. I'm sure you've heard of him."

"Master forger, counterfeiter, and bur-
glar," said Chief Bruno. "And just *when* is
he supposed to have stolen the document?"

"Sometime last night, I expect," replied
Fritz.

"Not!" said Sister. "He would have set off

the silent alarm when he broke into school! Just like we did tonight!"

Chief Bruno shook his head. "I didn't install that alarm until this morning," he said. "Remember?"

"If you think I'm lying," said Fritz, "all you have to do is prove that Grizzinski wasn't anywhere near the school last night."

"Very cute, Fritz," said the chief. "You know how hard it is to prove that something *didn't* happen. What makes it even tougher is that Phil Grizzinski lives way out by the tracks, north of the city, where nobody ever sees him come or go." He turned to the Bear Detectives and said glumly, "I'm afraid they've got us, cubs."

"That's ridiculous!" cried Ferdy. "Fritz Braun is a convicted forger who had the perfect opportunity to forge and steal the Grizzington document. We even found him with the stolen document! And I'm sure he hasn't a shred of evidence that this Grizzinski fellow did it."

"You're quite clever, son," said Fritz, with a sleazy smile. "But I'm afraid you have a lot to learn about Bear Country's system of justice. Ralph and I are the *accused* in this case. *You* have to *prove* that we're guilty. *We* don't have to prove anything."

"Gosh, that's right!" said Brother. "I remember that from Mr. Dweebish's class in Foundations of Democracy. *Innocent until proven guilty.*"

"I'm afraid so," said Chief Bruno. "We can't disprove their theory. And we need more evidence to prove ours. Evidence that even a thorough police investigation won't turn up."

"You see, son?" Fritz said to Ferdy, his smile turning smug. "Even your chief of

police agrees with me." And then he winked.

"He winked at me!" cried Ferdy.

"I did not," said Fritz calmly. "I just had something in my eye."

"Yes, he did!" insisted Ferdy. "That's evidence of guilt! We can convince the jury! We'll tell them how Fritz winked!"

Fritz chuckled. "A wink?" he said. "You call that *evidence?* My lawyer, Bombastic Bearskin, would have a field day with it."

Sadly, Chief Bruno nodded.

"Well, Chief," said Ralph, "it looks like Phony Phil Grizzinski committed the perfect crime."

"You mean, *you and Fritz* committed the perfect crime," said Chief Bruno. "*Almost,* that is. At least we got you for possession of stolen property. Cuff 'em, Marguerite!"

Chapter 14
As Good as Old?

Minutes later, Ralph Ripoff and Fritz the Forger were safely behind bars at the Beartown Police Station. Chief Bruno had radioed for a paddy wagon, then driven the Bear Detectives to Bear Country School to return the George Grizzington document to its rightful place in the teachers' lounge. They were met there by Mr. Dweebish and Grizzly Gus.

Chief Bruno told the history professor what had happened at Grizzly Mansion, then left for the police station. As Gus reattached the document to the bulletin board, the cubs talked with Mr. Dweebish.

"It's a shame we can't get Ralph and Fritz convicted of stealing the document," said Brother. "They won't get much of a sentence for possession of stolen property."

"Well," said Mr. Dweebish, "at least we got the document back in time for the bicentennial."

"And found out why the last three letters of the signature were written with a fountain pen," Ferdy pointed out.

"Quite true," said Mr. Dweebish. "It goes to show how carefully the crime was planned. And it very nearly worked."

"I still don't get it," said Sister. "I don't understand why a jury would believe that phony story about Phil Grizzinski stealing the document."

"But a jury doesn't have to believe it to

keep those two from being convicted," said Mr. Dweebish. "In fact, not even a single juror has to believe it. All Fritz's lawyer has to do is persuade one juror out of twelve that his client's story *might* be true. It's called *reasonable doubt*. If even one juror

has a reasonable doubt about the accused being guilty, he or she must vote against a conviction. As for the Phil Grizzinski story, it could have happened that way. Not very likely, I'll admit. But it *might* have. There's no evidence to disprove it. So it stands to reason that once Bombastic Bearskin got through with the jury, at least *one* of them would have a reasonable doubt about Fritz and Ralph's guilt."

Sister shook her head. "It just doesn't seem right to let someone get away with burglary," she said. "Especially someone who almost ruined the bicentennial." The other cubs nodded in agreement.

"I know it doesn't," said Mr. Dweebish. "Of course, it's never *right* when someone gets away with a crime. But maybe I can help you all understand why this has happened." He gestured at the bulletin board, where Grizzly Gus was putting the finishing touches on the corners of the document. "Don't forget that it was George Grizzington himself, along with our other forebears, who designed our system of justice to work this way."

Sister frowned. "But why would they want to protect criminals?" she asked.

"They didn't," said Mr. Dweebish. "They wanted to protect everyone else."

"From what?" asked Brother.

"From the great power of our very own government," said Mr. Dweebish. He pointed to the document on the board. "Do

you see what George Grizzington wanted to discuss that night, two centuries ago? *Life, liberty, and the purfuit of happineff*—er, I mean, *pursuit of happiness*. By *liberty*, he

meant the personal freedom of each and every one of us. He wanted to protect us from having our liberty unjustly taken away by the government. And that's why, to this day, if our government wants to put someone in prison, it must prove, beyond a reasonable doubt, that he or she has committed a crime. But what is a reasonable doubt? That's something that we all must decide for ourselves."

The cubs were silent for a moment. Then Brother said, "Wow. I never imagined that what happened tonight could have anything to do with *history.*"

Just then Gus stepped back from his handiwork and said, "There! As good as new. Or maybe I should say, 'As good as *old.*' "

The cubs laughed. So did Mr. Dweebish. But then he said, "Actually, Gus, I think you

were right the first time. After all, the ideas of George Grizzington and our other forebears are still going strong today. If they weren't, we might not be having a bicentennial at all."

"Hmmm!" said Gus. "That's something to think about."

Indeed, the Bear Detectives thought about it all the way home in Mr. Dweebish's car. And the next day, they couldn't help thinking about it again from time to time, right there in the middle of all the bicentennial festivities.

Stan and Jan Berenstain began writing and illustrating books for children in the early 1960s, when their two young sons were beginning to read. That marked the start of the best-selling Berenstain Bears series. Now, with more than one hundred books in print, videos, television shows, and even Berenstain Bears attractions at major amusement parks, it's hard to tell where the Bears end and the Berenstains begin!

Stan and Jan make their home in Bucks County, Pennsylvania, near their sons—Leo, a writer, and Michael, an illustrator—who are helping them with Big Chapter Books stories and pictures. They plan on writing and illustrating many more books for children, especially for their four grandchildren, who keep them well in touch with the kids of today.